# Disney's
# My Very First Winnie the Pooh™

## A,B,C with Pooh

Cassandra Case

Illustrated by Orlando de la Paz and John Harmon

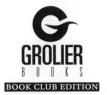

GROLIER BOOKS

BOOK CLUB EDITION

Based on the Pooh stories by A.A. Milne
(copyright The Pooh Properties Trust).

Printed in the United State of America.

First published by Disney Press, New York, NY
This edition published by Grolier Books, ISBN: 0-7172-8870-6
Grolier Books is a division of Grolier Enterprises, Inc.

Christopher Robin is sad
This blustery autumn day.
He lost his ABC blocks.
They seem to have blown away!

All his Hundred-Acre friends
Help search for the missing blocks.
They look in fields, under stumps,
And inside old honey crocks.

Lucky Pooh Bear finds the first—
He lets out a happy cry.
"A and B are in a tree!
I wonder if they can fly?"

Turning the teapot over,
Piglet lets out a loud squeak,
C and D come bouncing out —
Good thing he gave it a peek!

Eeyore stops his complaining
When he just happens to see
E and F come drifting by
In a pond—as plain as can be.

Owl is doing some thinking,
Pacing up and down his floor.
G and H give him a shock,
Blowing in through his front door.

Tigger is his happy self,
Bouncing and singing until
I and J get in his way,
And Tigger takes quite a spill!

Kanga opens her curtains
And sees two things she knows well.
"Look what I found on the ledge,
Cries Kanga, "It's K and L!"

"This jar was empty before,
But now it's not!" says Pooh,
"M and N are in the pot—
It's just too good to be true!"

But Gopher is not happy.
While sleeping snug in his bed,
O and P came tumbling in,
And hit him smack on the head!

Roo, with a skip and a jump,
Crosses the stream all alone.
Q and R give him some help,
For each makes a stepping stone!

Eeyore just stands and wonders—
"Can I believe what I see?
I came here to eat some hay,
But instead find S and T!"

Piglet goes to his garden,
Certain that he cannot fail.
Of course he finds U and V
Pouring right out of his pail!

Something for Kanga and Roo
Is not their usual mail.
Did the wind send W?
It makes a wonderful tale!

"Can this be?" exclaims Rabbit.
"These two are very strange fruit.
Could I have grown X and Y?
No, no! But aren't they cute?"

"We're not done yet," says Pooh-Bear.
"What's this by an old tree root?"
He picks up what he has found,
And Z falls out of a boot!

Christopher Robin is glad,
And all of his friends are, too!

They stack the blocks—A to Z—
Singing "A…B…C…" Can you?